Abigail and the Tropical Island Adventure

Tali Carmi

Abigail and the Tropical Island Adventure

Tali Carmi

Abigail and the Tropical Island Adventure\Tali Carmi

First edition – 02/2015

ISBN-13: 978-1508699132

ISBN-10: 1508699135

Contact information: tbcarmi@gmail.com

Author website: www.thekidsbooks.com

Twitter: @tbcarmi

To my beloved children

It was a cold, rainy day so Abigail could not play outside. She looked out the window and thought about the wonders of weather. When there is winter on one side of the world, there is summer in another place.

There are places in the world where there is never winter
Abigail remembered and thought how much fun it could be
to live in such a place.

She smiled to herself while thinking of her adventures
around the world, and felt so lucky to have that magical
bicycle her inventor grandpa built for her.

She went to her room, opened the magical book and saw amazing pictures of tropical islands, beautiful sandy beaches and palm trees. She imagined how she would take a walk on the beach and the sun would caress her face. Oh, how she missed summer.

Abigail said the magical words, "Take me there let me see; show me where I want to be," and immediately found herself flying over a beautiful island archipelago. She could already see the clear blue sea and beautiful green islands.

Abigail landed next to a big coconut tree, she knew it was not safe to stay under that kind of tree, because a coconut could fall on her head without warning, so she decided to have a walk on the beach and breathe the fresh, salty air.

A young girl, holding a huge shell beside her ear, was standing there quietly with a big smile on her face. When she saw Abigail she introduced herself: "Hi, my name is Lelei, who are you?" The shell was as big as her head and Abigail wondered why she was holding it next to her ear.

"I'm Abigail," Abigail replied, "I came on my magical bicycle from far away."

"Do you want to hear something Amazing?" asked Lelei. "Put this shell close to your ear."

"Wow, I hear the sea inside!" Abigail said with surprise. "How come?"

"The shell absorbs noises around it and it sounds like the sea," explained Lelei.

"I love to learn new things!" said Abigail with joy, and Lelei was happy that she taught Abigail something new. "Today is my birthday; my parents are throwing me a party, would you like to come?" asked Lelei.
"Yes! I would love to, thank you for inviting me," said Abigail, already excited.

Suddenly, they saw a man coming out of the sea with a bag made of fishing net. It was full of oysters that he collected from the bottom of the sea.

"Hello Lelei, and to you as well, girl" he said.

"Abigail, meet Maru, he is a professional pearl diver," said Lelei. Maru opened one of the oysters and inside they saw a beautiful, shiny pearl.

"The pearl is created by the oyster," explained Maru, "and we were lucky to find it because they are very rare."
"That is amazing, and they really are beautiful," said Abigail.

The girls were heading to the birthday party when Abigail saw a very strange thing in the clear water. "What is that?" she asked.

"That's a starfish," Lelei told her.

"That's a fish?" Abigail wondered aloud.

"No," laughed Lelei, "this is a beautiful creature in a star shape but the name is misleading, it's not a fish."

Abigail and Lelei reached the party area and saw Lelei's mother and her friends. "Lelei, there's a problem," said her mom, "the power station was damaged yesterday by the storm, and the power lines are down. We will not have lights for the party until it's restored."

Lelei was very sad, but Abigail already had an idea, after all, she was the granddaughter of a resourceful inventor. She remembered what Grandpa taught her about electricity, and said, "We can make electricity by connecting wires from my bike paddles to a dynamo and this will turn the lights on."

Abigail turned the paddles with as much strength as she could, and the paddles continued turning with the help of the magical bicycle. The light turned on and the celebration started. Lelei was very happy and her friends began cheering with joy and enjoying the party.

"Abigail, thank you so much, you saved my party," said Lelei at the end of the evening. "Take this gift as a token of appreciation. It's a traditional island dress."

"Thank you so much," said Abigail. "It's already dark and I must go home now, but I will come to visit you again."

"Mother, see this lovely dress that I got from my friend Lelei on a tropical island," said Abigail when she got back home.

"Abigail, Grandma told me that you have an evolved imagination," said Mom, "but this dress is so special, I wonder where it really came from." Abigail laughed out loud; she knew it was not only her imagination.

Thank you!

This book has been created with love and joy
and it is very important for me to hear
what you think about it.
Please press the link below and leave a review.
Your thoughts mean a lot to me.

Lots of love
—Tali

My dear readers,

Thank you for purchasing *Abigail And The Tropical Island Adventure*, the 4th book of *Explore the World Children's Books* series. I really enjoyed writing about this little girl and her adventure at the tropical island. I hope you too enjoyed it.

I appreciate that you chose to buy and read my book over some of the others out there. Thank you for putting your confidence in me to help educate and entertain your kids.

If you and your children enjoyed *Abigail And The Tropical Island Adventure* and you have a couple of spare minutes now, it would really help me out if you would like to leave me a review (even if it's short) on Amazon. All these reviews really help me spread the word about my books and encourage me to write more and add more to the series! If you'd like to read another one of my children's books, I've included more information on the next page for you.

Sincerely yours,

Tali Carmi

Other books by Tali Carmi

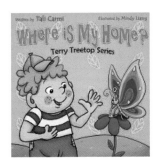 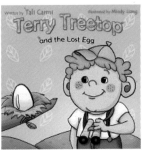 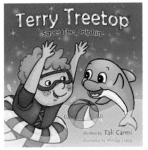 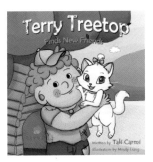

CPSIA information can be obtained at www.ICGtesting.com
Printed in the USA
LVIW01n1418020316
477478LV00021B/86